CHARLIE MEADOWS

For Ferd Monjo R.H.

For Mum & Dad M.B.

Text copyright © 1984 by Russell Hoban
Illustrations copyright © 1984 by Martin Baynton
All rights reserved, including the right to reproduce this
book or portions thereof in any form.
First published in the United States in 1984 by
Holt, Rinehart and Winston, 383 Madison Avenue,
New York, New York 10017.

Originally published in Great Britain by Walker Books Ltd.

Library of Congress Cataloging in Publication Data

Hoban, Russell.
Charlie Meadows.
(Russell Hoban's Ponders series)
Summary: While delivering the news to the other field
mice, Charlie Meadows, who loves dancing with his shadow
in the moonlight, narrowly escapes being eaten by the owl.
[1. Mice—Fiction. 2. Owls—Fiction. 3. Animals—
Fiction] I. Baynton, Martin, ill. II. Title. III. Series.
PZ7.H637Ch 1984 [E] 84–679
ISBN: 0-03-069502-3
First American Edition
Printed in Italy
1 3 5 7 9 10 8 6 4 2

ISBN 0-03-069502-3

CHARLIE MEADOWS

RUSSELL HOBAN

Illustrated by
MARTIN BAYNTON

HOLT, RINEHART AND WINSTON
NEW YORK

Charlie Meadows had a paper route.
His paper was an old and yellowed torn-off
scrap of headline. BLEAK OUTLO, it said.
Charlie carried it on a stick. When the other
meadow mice saw the paper coming they
knew that it was Charlie with the news and
weather.

Charlie got the weather from his grandmother. She had rheumatism and she always knew when it was going to rain. The news he picked up as he made his rounds. Charlie always made his rounds between midnight and three o'clock in the morning. Every time he went out his mother said to him, 'Look out for Ephraim Owl or *you'll* be in the news.'

Charlie always said he would be careful but he was not quite as careful as he might have been because he was too fond of moonlight. He especially liked the full-moon nights in winter when the shadows were black on the snow and the frozen pond creaked and his whiskers were stiff with the cold. Sometimes he would skate on the pond and on the frozen stream that ran through the meadow and the woods.

One full-moon night Ephraim Owl was sitting in a tall pine that overlooked the pond. There had just been a fresh snowfall and the ice on the pond was white under the moon.

Ephraim ruffled up his feathers and made himself bigger. 'WHOOHOOHOO!' he hooted and looked all around to see if anyone jumped up and ran.

'WHOOHOOHOOHOO!' he hooted again. Such a sudden sound, so strange! Even Ephraim wasn't sure if he had made it or if it had leaped out of the night all by itself.

When Charlie heard the hooting he was in the shadow of the pines on his way from Poverty Hollow to Frogtown Stump. Up he jumped and ran out into the whiteness of the frozen pond. His little black shadow began to dance. It kept changing its shape and Charlie had to dance and change his shape with it. The shadow of his stick and paper grew long, grew short, spun around and around as he danced.

Down swooped Ephraim from the tall pine, down he swooped on silent wings with outstretched talons. Just as he was going to grab Charlie he drew back his talons and flew up again. He wanted Charlie for his supper, but he didn't want Charlie's little shadow to stop dancing. He liked the way it whirled and changed its shape. He flew low over the ice and tried to make his shadow do the same. It seemed the proper thing to do in the moonlight.

Around and around went Charlie's
shadow and Charlie, around and around
went Ephraim's shadow and Ephraim.
Ephraim's shadow got all mixed up with
Charlie's shadow and Ephraim became
confused.

He sat down suddenly on the ice while
everything went around and around him.
That was when Charlie noticed Ephraim for
the first time. He too became confused, he
stopped dancing and stood absolutely
still, trembling all over and
staring at Ephraim.

Ephraim looked at Charlie's paper. 'What's that?' he said.

'BLEAK OUTLO,' said Charlie.

'What's a BLEAK OUTLO?' said Ephraim.

'It's a paper,' said Charlie.

'I can see that it's a paper,' said Ephraim. 'But what does BLEAK OUTLO mean?'

'I don't know,' said Charlie. 'That's what it says on the paper.'

'How do you know that's what it says?' said Ephraim.

'My grandmother told me,' said Charlie.

'Oh,' said Ephraim.

Ephraim began to think of supper again. He stood up and ruffled up all his feathers and made himself big. He spread his wings and leaned low towards Charlie to show his ruffled-up back feathers and the tops of his wings so that Charlie could see how big he was. He snapped his bill and his yellow eyes stared straight at Charlie.

Charlie couldn't move. He stood there as if he were frozen to the spot, his little black shadow was perfectly motionless.

Ephraim looked at Charlie's shadow. 'Oh, well,' he said, 'never mind.' He made himself regular-size again. 'You watch it next time,' he said, and off he flew.

Charlie hurried on to Frogtown Stump. 'BLEAK OUTLO news and weather,' he said: 'warm spell coming, rain and fog.'

'What about the news?' said the Frogtown Stump mice.

'Ephraim Owl's out hunting by the pond,' said Charlie.

'That's not news,' said the Frogtown Stumpers.

'No,' said Charlie, 'I guess it isn't.'

He never told them what happened at the pond, he let that stay between him and Ephraim.